GHOSTS
of
LOOKOUT
MOUNTAIN

The Appalachians were here long before we came to these beautiful mountains, and they will be here long after we are gone.

Speaking of "gone," a lot of folks can't really let go when they're gone. These stories are accounts of some of those who can't seem to hang it up.

So much of American history is embodied in the one single mountain we call Lookout Mountain, and in the surrounding area.

The clashes between the Native Americans and the whites were only the beginning. The Revolutionary War impacted the area and also especially the Civil War. All of these circumstances contributed to this corner of America being an epicenter of violence.

All this has spawned a rich heritage of ghosts here.

This book is dedicated to all of the people who have lived around, traveled across, and in some cases, refused to leave Lookout Mountain. May your love and respect for the magnificence of this area and its part in American history live forever.

TABLE OF CONTENTS

FOREWORD

THEY DO EXIST!
(as told by the author's sister)

  I used to think that ghosts were simply things to make children's stories scary. To call me skeptical of such supernatural phenomena would have been a gross understatement.
Anyone thinking they'd seen a ghost must have a very vivid imagination, or else be borderline goofy. Then one afternoon I walked into my  den and met one myself, in what was one of the greatest shocks of my life.

We had lived in our home in Georgia for about a dozen years. Five years previously, we had converted the garage into a den. That afternoon, I was home alone, or at least that's what I thought. I had been to the utility room to check on clothes in the dryer, and was walking back to the front of the house. As I walked down the hallway and stepped down into the den, I was startled to see a

 strange lady standing in the middle of the room. She was of medium height and build, but her clothes belonged to a different era, possibly back in the 1950s. She had on a rust-colored shirtwaist dress with a full skirt like she was wearing a crinoline. Her hair was in a bouffant style that was popular during the 1950s period. There isn't an outside door in our den, so I couldn't imagine what this lady was doing in my home, or how she'd gotten there.

"May I help you?" I managed to stammer.

The lady turned to face me, and appeared as startled as I felt. That was when I noticed that I really couldn't see her feet, as there was a misty cloud starting right below her knees. Then I received a bigger shock, as she suddenly disappeared. She was standing there one second, then was totally gone the next.

I stumbled over to the couch and sat down, trying to digest what I had witnessed. The room was empty except for me. I got up and went to our front door. It was locked, as it normally was. I looked outside, and saw nobody. I checked the back door. Locked. I walked back to the den, but it looked the same as it typically did. That was when it really began to sink into my brain; I'd just seen a ghost. They DO exist! Suddenly the very basic foundations of my world felt quite shaky.

I wondered whether our house had been built over her original home place, and she was looking for it. There was also a story of a murder somewhere in our general area many years previously, so I wondered about that, too.

Then I realized what others no doubt experience, and that is the fact that people might not believe me. Would they think I was crazy, or making it up? Did I even dare mention it to anyone? Actually it was months before I got the nerve to tell anyone about the experience, and I'm still not sure whether they believed me or not. But I am now certainly convinced that, yes, ghosts, or some type of spirits, do exist!

PREFACE

The Appalachian Mountains, located in the eastern United States, extend 1600 north-south miles from Quebec to Georgia. The Appalachians are actually a system of long ridges divided into several ranges, averaging 3,000 feet, and rising to Mt. Mitchell (6,684 ft.) in the south and Mt. Washington (6,288 ft.) in the north. Although much cultivation and urbanization has occurred in some parts of the Appalachians, there are still many remote areas.

The most popular attraction for mountain hiking enthusiasts is the Appalachian Trail, a 2,100-mile hiking trail that winds through forested mountains from Springer Mountain in

Northern Georgia to Mount Katahdin, Maine. Called the AT by hikers, this trail crosses portions of fourteen states, and generally takes five to six months to complete.

These mountains are often called the answer to prayers of Nature lovers. From one end to the other of this long chain of majestic ridges is one site after another where visitors can partake of outdoor activities of many types, or simply relax and enjoy the extraordinary scenery.

"Historic" is also a popular word used to describe the Appalachian Mountains, as they have been home to many aspects of this country's most famous and infamous history. Many battles have been fought along these mountains. These include

battles against foreign countries, battles against the native Indians, and, unfortunately, battles against each other. There has been much blood shed along this chain of mountains, making them a source for many haunting tales.

Ghost stories seem to thrive on violence and the untimely demise of people, making this mountainous area a prime location for mystic legends.

One theory holds that these people/ghosts hang around to avenge their own deaths, have difficulty accepting the fact that they are actually dead, or are stuck in an unknown area between the living and the dead, not knowing how to move on to the after-death experience.

In any event, this mountainous area abounds with legends and handed-down accounts of ghost stories of every imaginable description. From apparitions, bizarre

 lights and sounds, sightings, and simply unexplainable occurrences, these stories take on a strange life of their own.

Of course it is irrelevant that these tales, as is true of most ghost stories, cannot be confirmed as factual. Most of these stories have been handed down from generation to generation, are local legends, or are simply hearsay. As in other gossip or rumors, it is more important for them to be interesting than true. It is also good to leave a lot of mystery in the interpretation to the readers.

The stories in this book are set in the southern end of the Appalachian Chain, just south of the Great Smoky Mountain National Park, around a 93 mile long mountain by the name of Lookout Mountain.

Lookout Mountain

Down along the southern end of the Appalachian Mountains is a long ridge known as Lookout Mountain. It is truly a history-lover's dream. Lookout Mountain has been greatly involved in American chronicles down through the years. There were battles fought along its peaks and plateaus during the Revolutionary War, the Civil War, and numerous skirmishes between the settlers and the Indians who lived there. The mountain has been in the middle of other aspects of history, some gallant and honorable, and some quite infamous.

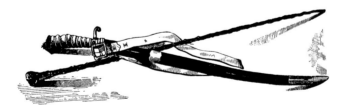

The extreme northern end of the mountain extends into the southeastern corner of Tennessee, and contains a portion near Chattanooga from which a person can gaze out upon parts of seven different states. This unusual panorama is from whence the mountain draws its name. The mountain extends more than eighty miles south and west of Chattanooga into northwestern Georgia and the northeastern strip of Alabama.

Only about three miles of the mountain are actually in Tennessee, with the next thirty-one in Georgia, and the final fifty stretching down into Alabama. Over 2000 feet high in places, the width varies from one to almost ten miles at times. The mountain has a sandstone cap that runs along the top of the mountain. Several hundred feet below that is a layer of shale nearly 400 feet thick. The rest of the mountain is limestone, and the erosion in the limestone resulted in the many caverns.

When the pilgrims arrived in America, the Appalachian Mountains were heavily populated with several Indian tribes. As the white man  encroached and settlements sprang up, there were many conflicts, and the Indians were slowly but surely forced to retreat. At the urging of several affluent newcomers, the federal government eventually allowed laws and treaties to be passed which made it impossible for the Indians to remain in their homelands.

Fort Payne, Alabama, was built as a place of internment and removal for the Indians who were forced to leave their lands and travel to a new home in Oklahoma. Fort Payne was one of the starting points for the forced marches in which the Indians were not only pushed aside, but totally relocated, with one of the most infamous atrocities being what is known as "The Trail of Tears."

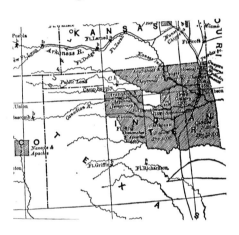

The Indians were rounded up and marched a thousand miles away to live on reservations set up in what was then considered the less inhabitable area of the country known as Oklahoma.

From the clashes between the Indians and the white men, there was much bloodshed, with many acts of violence from both sides. Then there was hostility of the fighting along that area during the Revolutionary War. Finally, the area was a hotbed of activity during the Civil War. With all of this violence, it is only natural that the supernatural made its own presence known, and there are many, many ghost stories that have been told and retold down through the years.

The Appalachian area is also the home of many limestone caverns along the mountains. Some of these caves have rooms large enough to hide a regiment of soldiers during the Civil War. Some of these caves have been explored for over fifty miles without finding the end. Some of these caves have never been explored. It has never been unusual to discover human bones during the explorations, as people became lost, disoriented, or injured, and could not get back to the outside world.

There is nothing as foreboding as to be far underground in a cavern and realize that anything known to man, and some things not yet known, may well be lurking around the very next bend, and they may not welcome intruders.

All of these things combine to make the mountain area a fruitful place for ghost stories. Massacred families, Indian warriors, war soldiers, and even spurned lovers still haunt the woods, caves, and settlements along Lookout Mountain. In this book we will explore a few of the yarns, legends, narratives, and other chronicles of the hauntings that have been experienced in the communities on and around Lookout Mountain.

The Crying Child

 When James and Clara King decided to build a vacation cabin near the small town of Mentone, Alabama, they were looking for a quiet, scenic getaway from the hustle and bustle of city life in Birmingham. They found what they thought was a perfect location and quickly purchased it.

 The ideal spot they found for their cabin was along the picturesque brow of Lookout  Mountain, right off the Desoto Parkway, midway between Fort Payne and Mentone, Alabama. The closest neighbors consisted of a large Boy Scout campground, and scattered cabins similar to what they wanted for themselves. The lot they purchased was about a half acre, two-thirds of which was heavily wooded. The back side of their lot dropped sharply down the side of the mountain, affording a splendid view of the valley far below. They decided that an A-frame cabin design, with a lot of glass, would be ideal for them.

Near the back of the lot, and exactly where they intended to build their cabin, they discovered the

remains of the abode of a previous tenant. There were several large stones where a fireplace and chimney had been, and an area of recessed flat stones that could easily be incorporated into a patio. They quickly assembled plans for their cabin and hired a crew to build it.

Problems were encountered almost immediately. Several of the construction workers quit after only a few days. They were always vague about why they quit, but one guy complained that he couldn't even light a cigarette at the site, as the flame on his lighter wouldn't stay lit. Others complained about somebody messing with their equipment, and even moving some of the rocks around after they had painstakingly placed them.

Although the construction took about twice as long as planned, the A-Frame was eventually completed, and the new owners eagerly drove over for their first weekend in it.

The very first night they spent in their new cabin, Clara was awakened shortly after midnight by the distinct  sound of a small child crying. By the time she woke James, the sound had stopped, and he attributed it to a wild animal. It had sounded so real and so close that Clara had difficulty getting back to sleep, but there was no repeat of the sound. The next morning, James was dismayed to see that two of the large stones had been moved over against the side of the house. With an effort, he managed to return the stones to their new position at the front of the patio.

That night, again shortly after midnight, both the Kings were startled awake by the unmistakable sounds of a small child crying out in terror. James immediately arose and searched the house, but the sound stopped, and its source could not be discovered. When James turned on the yard lights and stepped outside to check, the only thing he saw amiss was the fact that the two large stones had been moved again over against the house.

James assured Clara that it was probably the work of some pranksters, and possibly even a strange way of the neighbors welcoming them to the area.

Clara was not so sure, and decided to do some investigating before spending another night in that cabin. She drove into nearby Fort Payne, and with the assistance of the local historical society and a helpful librarian, discovered some interesting history concerning the spot where their cabin was located.

During the latter part of the Civil War, there was a family by the name of Harbison who had a cabin approximately where the new King cabin had been built. Jake Harbison joined the Southern army, but before he left home, he added a small stone safe haven adjacent to the fireplace. Appearing to be part of the wall,  it was actually a small compartment large enough for two or three people to hide. A story told of a small band of Northern soldiers marching through the area. They were half-starved, and pillaged any homes they ran across, searching for food and bounty. Coming upon the Harbison cabin, they broke inside, but found nothing of value. Aggravated, they set the cabin afire.

Unknown to them the Harbison lady and her small child had hidden themselves in the compartment by the fireplace, and it had no outside escape. As fire and smoke consumed the small cabin, the terrified screams of a small child rang out loudly. One of the Northern soldiers threw down his gun and ran back inside the raging inferno, attempting to rescue the crying child. His valiant attempt was in vain, and he perished in the fire, along with the two Harbisons.

Although Clara King couldn't be positive, the remnants of the Harbison cabin could have been the ones they discovered on the property where they built their cabin. The large stones could have been the ones used for the safe compartment by the chimney that eventually served as a death chamber for the Harbison wife and child. The screaming sounds that woke the Kings could have been the Harbison child.

In any event, the Kings never spent another night at their cabin. They put the place in the hands of a local realtor and never set foot there again. The cabin quickly sold, twice, but each time the new owners didn't stay. Most people are hesitant to admit that they have witnessed anything haunting or ghostly, so nobody knows for certain why the tenants quickly resold the property. Then, while vacant, the cabin built by the Kings burned to the ground late one night. By the time the fire was discovered, it was too late to save it. The cabin was completely destroyed, but nothing more than a foot from the exterior walls was damaged in the least. Two large stones stood against where one wall had been, but they didn't even show any smoke damage.

The lot remains unattended, but the "for sale" sign has long since vanished.

The Opera House

In the early part of the twentieth century, the area on Lookout Mountain
south of
Chattanooga,
Tennessee,
became a popular
retreat for
people living in
the northeast.
Vacation homes,
campgrounds, and
even retirement

homes began sprouting up everywhere, and tourism
became a booming business. Not only was the area
peaceful and scenic, but there were also hot springs,
caverns, and hiking trails to provide recreation.

Some enterprising individual decided that they needed a
little culture in Summerville, Georgia, and built an opera
house right in the middle of town. It was a huge success

for awhile, then, as interest dwindled, it became a movie theater for a few years, and eventually turned into a bed and breakfast facility. It is in this latter capacity that it began capturing the imagination of its visitors.

The Wainwright family first turned the facility into a bed and breakfast. It wasn't long until they noticed that people staying in Room 2D often cut short their visit. Finally one of the clients mentioned the noises late at night near that room. Upon being questioned, the guests reluctantly admitted that they were scared to stay in the room. Every night around midnight, there was the sound of someone pacing back and forth in the hallway outside the door to 2D. If the door was opened to check for the source of the noise, nobody was ever seen. The pacing sounds would suddenly stop as soon as the door was opened, but would resume shortly after the door was closed again.

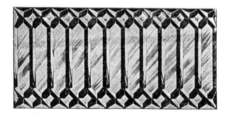

Another guest admitted hearing the pacing, but also the low murmur of someone talking. Not much of the dialogue could be discerned, but the person seemed to be talking to themselves, and sounded quite distressed. Again, if the door was jerked open, there was never anyone to be seen, and the sounds stopped abruptly.

After Mr. Wainwright at first ignored this nonsense, the rumors began circulating to the point of affecting his business, so he decided to do some investigating. From the local library he managed to find a sketch of the layout of the original opera house. The area approximately where room 2D was located had been a balcony overlooking the side of the stage. Another article mentioned a murder in the opera house. His curiosity thoroughly aroused, he continued to pursue the opera house history.

It seems that during one of the long-running plays at the opera house, the leading lady and the leading man became quite close; too close for the comfort of her spouse. The lady's husband, who was the director of the production, grew jealous. The lady was amused at his jealousy, and continued to flirt shamefully with the male actor. In a fit of rage one night, the director confronted, shot and killed the man after a performance. The lady, distraught at the turn of events, or possibly dismayed at losing her lover, fell to her death from that balcony later that same night. Her death was ruled a suicide, but her husband had been seen in the vicinity of the balcony shortly before her fall.

Surprisingly enough, the director was never charged with the murder of the actor, and disappeared shortly thereafter. The opera house was closed, and stayed locked and abandoned for many years.

Mr. Wainwright scoffed at the irrational idea of his establishment being haunted, but nevertheless, rumors continued, and business continued to decline. Deciding to squash the rumors, the Wainwrights were reputed to have stayed in room 2D themselves for one night, then left town the next day, leaving the bed and breakfast  establishment for sale. They didn't even take the time to pack more than a few clothes, leaving everything as it was.

The next owner kept Room 2D locked, never renting it out to anyone. It was only used for storage, but items left there were frequently moved around without any explanation. Eventually the door to Room 2D was paneled over and the only trace of its existence is a small window on the back side of the building. The window is boarded, but several of the townspeople have sworn they have seen light shining through the boards late at night.

Monteagle Mountain

A major thoroughfare cutting across from Chattanooga toward Nashville takes the traveler through a small town named Monteagle, Tennessee. This town is perched atop one of the last mountains on the west side of the Appalachian chain in that area. It is a tall mountain, and the west side drops off sharply. There is a nice modern

highway now leading the way out of Monteagle, down that west side of the mountain. This highway replaced the old road, which consisted of many sharp turns and descents, and was a nightmare for the large amount of commercial truck traffic using it. Even experienced drivers, who knew to go down that stretch in a low gear with great caution, occasionally lost control, and the lucky ones managed to jump clear of their cabs before they plummeted over the precipice.

This death trap of a mountain road was even featured in the Smoky and the Bandit movies as the place where the Bandit made his reputation and became famous for bringing his rig down that stretch safely when his brakes failed.

(Note: In 1964 this author made several trips down the old road driving a 1964 Pontiac GTO, one of the best handling cars of its era. Being young and foolish, I did it just for fun. Even knowing what to expect, and driving with some caution, I never failed to have at least one scary moment during the descent.)

Peering down over the edges of some of these hairpin

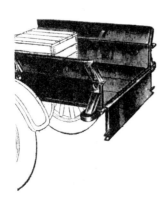

curves, past the damaged guardrails, one could frequently see pieces of trucks or trailers at their final resting places far below. Many times it was simply not feasible to try to drag the twisted remains back up the mountain, so they were just abandoned where they finally came to rest.

There were a couple of truckstops at the top of the mountain, and one right at the base of the mountain. While taking a rest and drinking coffee, many stories were told, but one of them stood out from the rest. This story was usually told by a young driver who had just made his first trip down that mountain road.

Strangely enough, the stories were very consistent, and not embellished with the retelling as so many stories are. Without fail, the drivers would relate how they were about halfway down the mountain, thinking that they had everything under control, when suddenly a figure appeared in the middle of the road. The figure was a man, dressed in light blue overalls and wearing a black cowboy hat, and he was always waving his arms furiously, as if to flag them down. Naturally the driver instinctively braked, and automatically downshifted another gear, and the figure promptly disappeared. Immediately the driver realized that he was moving into an even sharper turn than he'd seen

before, and that last downshift was what had kept him from running off the road and tumbling toward the valley far below.

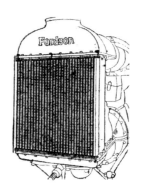

Whenever this story was told,

there was usually an older driver sitting there listening. He'd just chuckle and say, "That was just old Cowboy Lewis. He went over that curve to his death about twenty-five years ago. It was such rough terrain to get to where he wound up, and what with the fire and all, they supposedly just buried him there on the spot. Every few years he's been seen warning some unsuspecting young driver ever since."

The Mystery in Ruby Falls Cave

   While drilling for an elevator shaft above Lookout
Mountain Cave, another cavern was discovered in 1928.

What began
as a small
passageway
about 18
inches high
and about
four feet
wide quickly
opened up
into large
chambers,
with openings branching off in many directions. The new
cave, higher up the mountain than Lookout Mountain Cave,
contained most of the features of the more well-known
types of cave formations, including stalactites,
stalagmites, columns, drapery, and flowstone. But the

most stunning discovery was a 145 foot waterfall at the end of one large chamber.

The stream for the falls, 1120 feet underground, is fed by both rainwater and natural springs. The water eventually feeds into the Tennessee River.

The falls were named Ruby Falls, and the cave, Ruby Falls Cave, after the wife of the man who discovered them. The possibility of utilizing this marvelous waterfall as a tourist attraction was immediately recognized. It simply required a more accessible opening. There was also the possibility of other wonders hidden in the cavern.

Prior to World War II there were several popular legends associated with the cavern. These were never substantiated, and if they were made up to increase tourist traffic, that seemed to have worked. Around the 1950s the stories stopped being told as often. I, personally,

was told these stories by a former tour guide in the middle 1960s. Whether pure gossip or true, they do have a certain credibility about them.

According to one legend, one of the early explorers of the cave was a man by the name of Lomax. A veteran of many cave explorations, he was hired to discover what other treasures Ruby Cave might have. He squeezed through a small slot along one wall and found that it immediately opened into a room-size chamber. That soon led to an even larger chamber, with several smaller chambers branching off from it. In his enthusiasm, Lomax stayed much longer than he had planned, and was deep in the labyrinth when his light failed. Suddenly he was alone in a pitch-black cavern, with no sense of direction.

When Lomax failed to reappear in a reasonable timeframe, a search party was dispatched into the cavern opening. Their yells echoed back without any responses. Not sure exactly which direction Lomax had gone, the search party looked for several hours before discovering some trail markings that Lomax had made, and finally stumbled upon the lost explorer. He was sitting along a wall in a small chamber, staring straight ahead, unable to speak coherently, and had apparently been unable to reply to their summons. As they led him out of the cavern, he kept mumbling a warning to them about not going farther into the cavern.

Lomax was taken to a nearby hospital for examinations, and he slowly came back to his senses. At that point he refused to discuss what he had seen; only that he wouldn't go back in there. By the following day, every hair on his head had turned solid white. Within a week he had packed up all of his belongings and left the area, never returning to Ruby Falls Cave, and never explaining what had happened to him in the darkened cavern.

The narrow opening that Lomax had squeezed through was eventually widened, and when guided tours began being taken down into the cavern, they ventured into the chambers that Lomax had first explored. These tours were spooky for a couple of reasons. First, the tour guides spoke of there being ancient human bones uncovered in one of the chambers, although nobody knew how they got there, as no other opening to the outside had ever been discovered. Then there was another incident. As is popular on tours in caverns, the guide would pause along the trail and extinguish all lights, just to  show the people how dark it could get. Too many times when this happened, one or more of the tourists became terrified because they felt icy fingers touching their necks. When the lights were immediately turned back on, there was never anyone standing close to them. This always occurred in the same small chamber, so this chamber was eventually sealed off in the 1940s and not used any more on the tours. No one presently connected with the cave knows exactly where the mystery chamber is located.

Was there a connection between whatever had frightened Lomax half to death, the bones, and the feeling of icy fingers? The answer may still be lurking in a closed off chamber, somewhere deep inside Lookout Mountain.

The Lost Regiment

There was a lot of activity along Lookout Mountain during the Civil War. High up on the brow of the mountain were many great strategic locations, looking down over several paths traveled by both armies. As such, there were many skirmishes to obtain and to hold some of these places. The rugged terrain on each side of  the long mountain made for treacherous travel, both from the natural obstructions made by nature and from hidden enemy soldiers. There were also many caverns scattered along the mountain, providing great hiding places for those with knowledge of their locations. This all led to the establishing of dangerous, but advantageous campgrounds.

Those unfamiliar with the terrain, however, could easily become disoriented, especially in the darkness. This happened to a small band of Northern soldiers near the current town of Blanche, Alabama. They had been cut off from their main regiment during a particularly fierce battle near Adamsburg. Scared, wounded, and frustrated at being separated, they began to scramble along the eastern side of the mountain, trying to move north. They immediately began encountering enemy troops and unfriendly locals, causing them to retreat, scatter, and then regroup to continue their journey.

Soon there were only seven of them left together, as the others had been caught, shot, or scattered. As any

skilled woodsman has learned, wandering around in the woods lost, a person tends to travel in a large circle. This was the case with this small band. In the darkness and rain, they could not keep their bearings straight, and as they wandered around, were sighted, or heard, near the Blanche community at least three times during the night. They were last seen walking toward the southwest, into particularly nasty terrain. There were sinkholes and shear cliffs that were difficult to see until right on top of them. On the lower side of the mountain there was a well traveled path, but they apparently never reached it. None of the seven were ever accounted for.

However, beginning a few years after the war ended, and periodically ever since, there have been people near Blanche who have been witnesses to a strange phenomenon. To this day, it always occurs late on a rainy night, but the people claim that they clearly hear sounds of voices and marching in the distance.

Various people have described the sounds as people wailing, crying, or cursing. The events never last but a few minutes, as the sounds quickly fade into the distance.

Investigations have never found the source of the noises; however several times there have been footprints discovered the following mornings. These prints appear to be made by several men in boots, walking across the fields. The footprints seem to start from nowhere, continue for several hundred feet, and then suddenly end abruptly.

The local people simply refer to it as hearing the lost regiment still wandering along the mountain, searching for a destination they never found.

Moonshine Mountain

There is an isolated cove cut deeply into Lookout Mountain near the town of Trenton, Georgia, which has an interesting history. Starting during the 1920s and continuing for years, this cove was the site of the infamous Stover Still. Several generations of the Stover

family made their living running a still there.

By pure luck, one of the Stover kids discovered a small cave high up on the side of a sheer bluff. It could only be accessed from above, and that was by climbing down a rope. It afforded a clear view of much of the surrounding area, making it quite difficult for anyone to sneak up on it.

This cavern contained a small underground stream which passed through the cave, but not out of it. Thus there was no trickle of water going over the bluff to give away the location. Of course the Stovers immediately recognized the possibilities. They had been running moonshine stills for several years, but it was a constant hassle hiding the stills from the feds. Just when they got a good still set up, here would come the feds nosing around, and they'd have to relocate quickly.

When the Stover kid came home telling about the cave he'd discovered, the older folks didn't pay much attention at first. There were lots of caves around. But when he described the stream flowing through, but not out of the cave, ears became more attentive.

With a little investigating and some innovative design, the Stovers soon had a moonshine still set up in that little cave. Accessed above by a rope ladder, which was easily carried away or hidden, and the opening of the cave obstructed by branches, it seemed to be a perfect location. One of the dead giveaways of a moonshine still is the smoke that comes from cooking the mash. Many a revenuer has traced a plume of smoke in the middle of nowhere to a moonshiner cooking up a batch of brew. The Stovers, recognizing that drawback, came up with an ingenious solution. They ran a pipe down into the stream where it disappeared into the cavern wall. They fed the pipe for as far as they could, and then

hooked up their "cooker" to vent into that pipe. Wherever the smoke would eventually get to the surface, it was apparently dissipated and far away from their still.

To be on the safe side, they would station a guard up above the cave, and another one far down the mountain side. These guards would use lights at night and mirrors during the day to signal each other. Any sign of revenuers, and they would shut down the still and disperse, long before the feds could get close to them.

Everything seemed perfect, and in fact, worked flawlessly for several years. As is often the case, greed eventually became their downfall. One of the in-laws got on the outs with them and told all he knew to the Garner family. The Garners were also moonshiners, but not nearly as prosperous at the Stovers, as they kept getting caught. This meant some members of their clan were usually away for extended periods in jail.

The Garners decided to take over the cave as their own, and amassed a small army of their family. The Stovers got wind of the scheme, and amassed a small army of their own. Thus, early one morning there began an earnest siege. The Garners were determined to acquire the cave, and the Stovers were just as determined to defend it.

Meanwhile, the revenuers also heard of the brewing feud and staked out the general area where they suspected it to happen. The fighting was fierce and brutal, as neither side

was interested in taking any prisoners. The revenuers soon homed in on the exact location, but simply hung back and watched as the two moonshining factions wiped each other out.

It did, in fact, eventually get down to only one surviving fighter, and he was badly wounded and later died. Thus, the illegal liquor business suddenly went kaput in that area.

There was a big stink over what the feds didn't do, did do, or should have done to stop the bloodshed. Nobody was left to stand trial, nor to continue running the still.

Besides, its location had been totally compromised by the fighting.

A few months later, people began telling of seeing a light up on the mountain about where that still was located. In the daylight there was never a trace found where anyone could have been up there. Still periodically to this day, it is quite common for what appears to be a lantern moving around that location. Some people claim to have heard the occasional shot, and the sounds of people yelling coming from that direction.

One brave local boy went up on the mountain one night when he saw the light. As he  approached the base of the cliff, two bullets pierced a tree beside of his head, although he never heard the sound of a gunshot. That was enough of a warning for him, and his account of the incident was sufficient for others to leave well enough alone.

It is still common for a light to be seen up there. The recurring phenomenon is simply attributed to one of the moonshiners' ghosts, still trying to take control of the cavern.

The Ghost of Mr. Bumpas

There was a little community a few miles outside of what is now called Rising Fawn, Georgia, which was considered remote even by the mountain folk. The nearest post office was at a general store in Trenton, several miles to the north. There wasn't a paved road

leading to it until sometime in the 1980s. It did have some fertile land, however, and was settled in the late 1800s by a small farming group who were of predominantly German heritage. There were a few slaves who, after the Civil War, stayed around and became sharecroppers. A sharecropper works the land, is usually given a place to live, and splits the resulting crop profits with the landowner.

Eventually the black folk either died off or moved away, leaving one old sharecropper by the name of Bumpas. As Mr. Bumpas grew too old to actually do the heavy work in the fields, he began doing minor odd jobs around the

farms to pay for his upkeep. He lived in a small house on the Carr farm, all alone, without any known relatives left alive.

The community never had a church of any particular denomination; they just pitched in and built a church that they all attended. Mr. Bumpas became the church custodian, and that in due course became his major function. Although the doors of the church didn't even have locks for several years, when they were finally installed, Mr. Bumpas had the only keys. He always had the church open, fired up the stove to pre-heat the building in the winter time, and tidied up and closed the church after everyone else had gone home. Whenever the first person arrived at the church, they could be assured that they would hear the humming of Mr. Bumpas. Humming while he worked was a habit that he'd had for years, and everyone had grown to expect it. That was just part of Mr. Bumpas. The house where he lived was near the church, and by cutting across a field, he could be from one to the other within minutes.

The preacher during that time was T.D. Heinz, a self-taught, but knowledgeable scholar of the Bible. Reverend Heinz noticed that Mr. Bumpas would hang around outside the church, usually under a window near the front of the church, listening to the sermons. This was around 1950, and in Georgia the whites and the blacks didn't mix. Everything was separate, and particularly churches. However, Reverend Heinz realized that there was no way for Mr. Bumpas to go to a black church, because there weren't any within miles. So, without a second thought, he told Mr. Bumpas that he was welcome to come inside and listen to the service.

Mr. Bumpas wasn't sure that was a good idea, but with colder weather approaching, he gave in, and began stepping inside the door and standing in a back corner during the service. One of the other church members promptly set a chair back in that corner and declared it the Bumpas Chair.

Early one spring, a sudden storm came up, and knowing that the church windows were up, Mr. Bumpas started across the field to close them before it rained inside the church. Unfortunately, a bolt of lightning struck him dead before he reached the church.

The saddened community buried Mr. Bumpas in the little cemetery behind the church. Nobody had the heart to move Mr. Bumpas's chair from the corner, so there it remained.

Almost immediately, the people discovered that Mr. Bumpas might not have been ready to leave them. At different times, and always when they were in the church alone, several different members distinctly heard the sound of Mr. Bumpas humming. It wasn't uncommon for a shadow of a man to be seen through a church window, when the church would turn out to be vacant. Any trash left on the floor of the sanctuary would mysteriously be swept up in the corner beneath Mr. Bumpas's chair.

But the strangest thing of all happened during another storm. A tree toppled over, crashing through the back corner of the church's roof. This back corner housed a storeroom where most of the church literature was stored. When the church members came to the church to survey the damage, they expected all of the songbooks and other literature to be soaked and ruined. Instead, to their amazement, all of the books and papers were neatly stacked over against a wall, out of reach of the rainfall. None of it was damaged in the least. Everyone gave credit to Mr. Bumpas for once again taking care of them.

These things became so common that nobody thought much about them. But as their community became more accessible and more populated, they eventually built a new church building. Everyone assumed that the ghost of Mr. Bumpas would move right over to the new building; they even moved his chair over there. However, after the older building was torn down, there were no more unexplained events, as Mr. Bumpas apparently finally decided that it was time to rest.

Civil War Mail Drop

Not far from the town of Sulphur Springs, Alabama, was a major trail used by the soldiers during the Civil War. At various times, both the Northern and Southern armies marched along this trail.

Although Sulphur Springs wasn't much of a town at that time, there was a small general store, and it also served as a post office for those parts. As such, both sides of the war chose to consider the store neutral, as soldiers from the North and the South used the post office to send mail back home. Although the North and the South had separate postal systems, it was common for them to swap mail.

Whenever troops were passing along the trail, it was customary for them to send couriers to the store, carrying letters from the soldiers to be mailed. Occasionally they might even send a wagon for supplies. By a gentleman's agreement, the store never stocked ammunition.

As is often the case, word doesn't always get around to all of the people concerned. Some Northern reinforcements had just arrived from Ohio, and the agreement about the postal run hadn't been explained sufficiently to them. One of the new Yankee soldiers was on patrol late one evening, and spotted a lone Rebel soldier riding hurriedly down the trail coming from Sulphur Springs. Without a moment's hesitation he raised his rifle and cut down the Rebel.

His pride in his first kill was quickly squashed when his superior officer learned about the incident. The Southern victim was a 14 year old Georgia boy hauling a bag of letters back to his companions. The Yankee captain, flying a white flag of non-aggression, took the body and the letters down the trail to the  encampment of the Southern soldiers, expressing his utmost dismay at the unfortunate episode.

Years after the end of the war, more settlers moved into the community, and it became a thriving little town.

The original store was torn down and a combination saloon and hotel was built there. Years later a motel was built on the spot.

For as long as anyone can remember, every few months a guest will mention being awakened in the middle of the night by the sound of a running horse. Several have even looked out their window and seen a small shadowy horseback figure galloping down the street, then he and his horse suddenly disappearing into thin air.

The old-timers simply nod their heads, as they are accustomed to the stories. They explain to the guests that it was only the Rebel boy from Georgia making a mail run.

Gate for Ghosts

Valley Head lies along the eastern side of Lookout Mountain, just north of Fort Payne. It was populated by the Cherokee Indians until they were forced to march west to Oklahoma on the Trail of Tears. As many other communities in the area, it was heavily traveled by both sides during the Civil War.

Although originally a farming community, it now boasts a thriving tourist industry.

On the outskirts of the community remains a farm that has been in the same family for  several generations. It sits right in the middle of where numerous skirmishes took place during the Civil War.

Between two of the fields there is a gate, and is only used to go from one field to the other. It isn't near a road or trail, but in the middle of the farm. The gate always remains latched, to keep the cattle in one field or the other.

About once a month, inexplicably, the gate will be found standing wide open. Just as strange, the cows never go through the gate when that happens. It is as if the cows know the gate isn't supposed to be open, or as some say, there is something else keeping them from going through. The latch on the gate is quite secure, and can't be rattled loose, but invariably it will be found wide open again.

The family legend is that the gate is opened by a troop of Civil War soldiers passing through. The legend goes on to say that it must be Yankee soldiers, as any good Southern boy would know to close a gate after you passed through it!

The Blood-stained Crypt

A few miles north of Chattanooga, Tennessee, and about eighty miles south of Knoxville, nestled close to the

Cherokee National Forest is a small town named Cleveland. While it is currently known for being the home of several major kitchen range manufacturers, there is a lesser discussed claim to fame in downtown Cleveland.

Shortly after the Civil War, around 1871, a young girl from one of the more prominent families of the city was tragically killed in a buggy accident. The distraught family had a beautiful white marble crypt erected in her honor at St. Luke's Episcopal Church near downtown. While this was prim and proper, it was only the beginning of a strange happening that has continued to the present time.

Almost immediately after the crypt was completed, pinkish red stains appeared on the side of the white marble. Quickly the people tried to remove the stains by scrubbing them with various cleansers, but the stains remained. In desperation they replaced the stained white marble, but the pinkish red stains reappeared straight away.

Then the story gets even stranger. Other members of the same family as the little girl also met tragic ends, and after each death the stains on the marble crypt grew larger and more prominent. Various treatments failed  to affect the blemishes, and soon the people stopped trying to remove them, and simply accepted the stains.

To this day the stains remain on the white marble crypt, and there has never been a satisfactory explanation as to their origin.

Indian Ghosts at DeSoto Falls

   Along the southern brow of Lookout Mountain is
beautiful DeSoto Falls State Park. Supposedly discovered
by the Spanish
explorer DeSoto,
the park lies a
few miles east of
Fort Payne,
Alabama, and just
south of Mentone,
Alabama. The
showplace of the
park is DeSoto
Lake, and the
fabulous DeSoto
Falls.

   Fed by the West
Fork of Little River, the water plummets into a small
canyon that it has carved out over the centuries. The 104

foot falls actually consist of a series of three falls, each unique and beautiful.

The dam above the falls was built by Authur Abernathy Miller in the middle 1920s to power a generator he had built. This generator provided electric power to Fort Payne, Mentone, Valley Head, and Collinsville, Alabama, as well as to Menlo, Georgia.

Although named after the Spanish explorer for "discovering" them, the falls had been well known and used by the Indians for centuries. There is also some speculation that Welsh explorers might have also been there some three hundred years prior to Desoto.

Regardless of who deserves credit for their discovery, the falls have been enjoyed, not only for their hydroelectric usefulness, but also for their exquisite beauty for many years by many diverse peoples.

One reason we know that the Indians were well aware of the existence of the falls is an old Indian legend concerning them. The story tells of a beautiful young Cherokee maiden, the daughter of the chief, who fell in love with a young brave named Young Hawk. Unfortunately, her father, the chief, favored another brave, who was a great hunter. The chief wanted his daughter to marry the hunter, and pressured her to do so.

Young Hawk decided to prove his bravery to the chief, and thereby win approval to marry the beautiful maiden. The site he chose was what we now know as DeSoto Falls.

The series of falls end in an elegant green pool, seeming peacefully calm contrasted with the ferocity of the tumbling waters. A vertical rock wall rises majestically along one side of the river at this point, standing high above the water. Young Hawk climbed to the top of this cliff as the tribe gathered on the far side of the river.

They watched in awe as the Indian brave hesitated only briefly, then dove from the cliff, dropping elegantly to the pool far below. Alas, therein lays the tragedy. Young Hawk died from a broken neck as a result of his dive.

The young maiden, of course, was heartbroken at the loss of her true love. She is said to have been seen many times thereafter sitting quietly on the cliff, staring into the serene pool of water in the river far beneath her.

As far as legends usually go, it would have been romantic if she had jumped from the cliff herself, sacrificing herself to the river that took her love from her. In this legend, however, she apparently married the brave of her father's choosing, and was content to simply visit the cliff site occasionally, pining for what might have been.

That's not quite the end of the legend, however. For at least the last hundred years there have been reports of

strange apparitions at the falls. Numerous people have reported seeing a face of a young Indian woman in the falls. It always occurs when the sunlight hits the curtain of water from the last falls in the series a certain way. Various people over the years maintain that a clear image of the young girl's face appears on the wall of water.

But that isn't all, either. A myriad of people have also witnessed a strange apparition in the pool below the falls. Many people over the years have claimed that when a stone was tossed from the high rocky cliff, the ripples created from its entry into the water produced a brief, but distinct face of a young Indian brave.

The Great Buffalo Rock

Along the southern brow of Lookout Mountain, east of Fort Payne, Alabama, and scattered around the Desoto State Park and Little River Canyon area are a large number of unusually enormous boulders. Some of them are as large as houses.

In fact Sallie Howard Memorial Chapel was built around such a boulder. Located adjacent to the DeSoto State Park, the chapel is still a popular tourist attraction. Half of the boulder is outside the church, and half of it is inside, making it look as though the boulder rolled right into the back of the building. The part of the boulder inside the structure forms a backdrop to the altar. This chapel was built by Colonel Milford Howard in 1937 as a tribute to his first wife, and is quite an impressive sight.

The Indians, always closely attuned to items of Nature, held these large boulders in awe. They used some of these huge boulders in some of their more important ceremonies. One boulder, resembling a gigantic buffalo head growing out of the side of a hill, was used in a hunting ceremony. Before debarking on their mission, each of the braves would climb atop the boulder and ask for a safe and successful hunt.

Legend has it that during one of these hunting ceremonies, a band of white trappers attacked the Indians, killing them all. To have such a ghastly action enacted in a very hallowed place, and especially during a sacred ceremony, was quite upsetting to the Indians. They quickly tracked down and eliminated the trappers.

Soon after the attack, someone noticed water seeping from the boulder. The moisture had never been present before the slaughter, but it continues, slowly dripping from the rock. The Indians declared that the Great Buffalo in the rock was weeping for the Indian braves. This seepage continues to this day, and tests have shown it to be as pure as any spring water ever found.

Also, late at night, a low moaning sound can sometimes be heard seemingly emanating from the rock itself. Most of the Indians believed that this was the buffalo, too, although there was also the belief that it was the ghosts of the dead braves, doomed forever to have their spirits captured inside the giant rock.

The Ghost Rocker

Rainsville, Alabama, situated in the northeast part of the state and to the west of Lookout Mountain, is named in honor of Will Rains, who opened an eight-by-twelve log general store at the crossroads there in 1902. The town was incorporated in 1956, and the population in 2000 was approaching four thousand.

The town was built at the crossroads of Alabama Highway 35 and Alabama Highway 75. It grew less important when Interstate 59 bypassed it by nine miles, giving way to nearby Fort Payne.

It currently has a number of businesses in the health care sector, and is famous industrially for the manufacturing of church furniture. It is also famous for a long-time resident ghost in the community.

There is a farmhouse on the outskirts of Rainsville that was built in the middle 1800s. Generations of the same family have lived in it since that time. It began as a simple log cabin, then as the original family prospered, more and more was added on until it became one of the finest homes in the region.

During the Civil War, as was the custom, the house was commandeered for headquarters by whichever side had

the upper hand at that particular time. One of the finer houses in the area was taken over for the general to use while in that vicinity. Since this was common practice, the family living there simply moved out for a few days or weeks until the soldiers moved on. Usually some money was paid to the homeowner for the use of their abode, but not always.

The family who lived in this house maintained neutrality throughout the war, being courteous, and being treated courteously by the occupying soldiers.

The house had a porch extending across the front and down both sides. There were two front doors opening onto the porch, and a back door from the kitchen opening onto one of the side porches.

During one of the battles, the young son of the Northern general was badly wounded. He was brought to the house and administered to, but lost his left leg below the knee. As the army moved on, traveling south, the young soldier was left at the house, as he was in no shape to travel. Before the Northern army returned, however, a regiment from the South moved into the area, and its general took the house as his headquarters.

The quandary of the young Yankee soldier was explained, and he was allowed to stay in the house. This curious action was one of many such occurrences in the South during that war. Often common courtesy and compassion overcame the normal conventions of war.

A couple of the family members were allowed to stay and care for the wounded  soldier. The only restrictions were that the soldier and the caregivers must come and go using the back door.

Complications set in and the soldier remained a semi-invalid, unable to travel. Meanwhile, he had fallen in love with one of the daughters of the family, and was less inclined to move on anyway.

Eventually the soldier married the daughter, and remained at the house. He spent many hours sitting on the front porch, rocking in a chair, and gazing out at the nearby mountainside.

As the Northern and Southern armies passed through, the soldier became a communication guide for both groups. He received and sent letters for soldiers on each side, and even wrote letters for some who were in need of help. His usefulness far outweighed his allegiance, so both armies trusted and befriended him.

About the time the war ended, the young man had a setback, as his wound became infected. Within a few days, his condition worsened, and he died, sitting in his rocking chair on the porch.

There was a family cemetery, so the young man was laid to rest in it. The next day someone noticed that the rocking chair on the porch that the man used was slowly rocking, though nobody was near it. At first it was thought that the wind was moving the chair, but there followed times when the air was as calm as could be, but that empty rocking chair would be moving.

The head of the family decreed that the chair should always be there on the porch, left empty, and if the ghost of the young soldier wanted to rock, that was fine with him.

To this day
there remains a
rocking chair on
that front
porch.
Occasionally the
empty chair will be seen moving slowly to and fro, as if someone is sitting in it, slowly rocking. The current residents of the house accept it. They don't fully understand it, but they don't fear it, and they are accustomed to it.

The Ghosts of Corpsewood Manor

  One of the more infamous haunting stories along Lookout Mountain involves a manorhouse near the towns of Trion and Summerville, Georgia. The ruins of Corpsewood Manor, also known as Devil Worshiper's Mountain, are located on Taylor Ridge in Chattooga County, about five miles east of Trion.

  Dr. Charles Scudder was a pharmacology professor at Loyola University in Chicago prior to moving to Georgia. Wanting to escape the rat-race of city life, he bought forty acres of mountain tranquility and built Corpsewood

Manor as his dream home. Life there was intentionally simple, with no electricity or running water in the house. There were, instead, kerosene lamps, generators, and a pump for water.

Scudder moved into Corpsewood Manor with his housekeeper, Joseph Odom, and two English Mastiff dogs, one of which was named, "Beelzebub." They grew much of what they needed, and used interest from a savings account to purchase whatever else they required. The life was just what Scudder had desired, and the men lived in Corpsewood Manor in relative comfort for about six years.

From all reports, the two men were extremely nice, polite, and friendly, but different from the other people in the community. Perhaps because of their intentionally austere lifestyle, maybe because they were considered "outsiders," or perhaps because of more valid reasons, the gossip began to spread concerning Corpsewood Manor.

Rumors abounded that the men grew and used marijuana, and they had a vineyard for the express purpose of making their own homemade wine on the premises. Perhaps fueled by the fact that one dog was called Beelzebub, the scandalmongers soon claimed the men were also avowed devil worshipers, and likely homosexuals, as well.

Typically, all of these rumors provided much gossip throughout the nearby communities. Of course none of these rumors set very well with the local people, especially a young man by the name of Kenneth Brock. Brock had been allowed by Scudder to hunt on the land surrounding Corpsewood Manor, and although Brock had not been inside the main part of the manor, he began to spread the claims that the house contained Satanic materials.

Brock declared that the place was filled with human skulls, pornographic artwork, and other heinous objects used in worshipping the devil, even though he had never actually set foot inside. Apparently nobody questioned how Brock knew so much about worshipping the devil. Privately, Brock told an older friend, Tony West, that he knew for certain that Scudder was wealthy and had money hidden in the "big fancy" house. The men of the manor "lived like kings," and seemed to have everything they wanted. Because the inhabitants of the house were evil, Brock felt justified in robbing them.

In December, 1982, Brock and West picked up Jody Wells, who was a cousin to West, and Wells' girlfriend, Teresa Hudgins, with the pretense of going to the manor to do drugs and drink free wine. Upon their arrival at Corpsewood Manor, Scudder welcomed them, and took them to an outbuilding to do drugs. Soon West and Brock jumped Scudder, tied him up, and demanded money. Scudder denied having any money in the house.

Wells tried to talk West out of continuing the robbery, to no avail. At this point, Wells and Hudgins decided that they would leave the building.

Brock went to the main house, found Odom, and repeated the demand for money. Again being denied that any money existed, Brock shot Odom and the dogs. Then he returned to get Scudder and brought him into the manor, thinking that seeing Odom dead would show that he meant business. Scudder was distraught to see his friend dead, but still denied having any money. West shot Scudder.

Wells and Hudgins had retreated to their car, but couldn't get it started. Meanwhile Brock and West searched the house, but found only a few nickels and dimes. There were some items of value, such as jewelry and silver dinnerware, but nothing substantial. There was a large golden harp which Scudder enjoyed playing, but it was too big to fit in the killers' car, so it was left behind.

Not being overly intelligent, Brock and West were immediately arrested and convicted of the killings. The house was left abandoned, but of course became a site of curiosity to the locals. As is the nature of such places, it was immediately labeled as haunted. However, there seemed to be some reasons to justify the label.

Before Scudder was killed, he'd painted a self portrait. The picture showed him bound and gagged, with bullet wounds visible, much as what actually happened to him.

Naturally people began to loot items from the unattended house. It became a popular routine for the younger set to explore the Corpsewood Manor property. Unfortunately, something bad quickly happened to these looters, without fail. For instance, a male cheerleader took a brick from the site. Within a few days, he fell during a cheerleading stunt, and was injured and paralyzed for life. Before much time passed, the manorhouse burned to the ground late one night. The cause of the blaze was never determined. Several of the firefighters who responded to the fire reported seeing a lone male figure at the edge of the fire, but whenever they moved closer to him, he'd disappear and reappear somewhere else.

When people visited the manor site, both before and after the fire, a strange uneasiness came over them. Almost everybody who visited the house felt it. There seemed to be an ominous presence of "something" watching them. People visiting at dusk reported seeing a pair of red eyes, similar to those from a large dog, staring at them from the ruins.

Various people over the years have reported hearing a harp playing from amidst the ruins. There have also been numerous reports of people seeing a man on the premises dressed in solid black clothing, but when approached, he always vanished.

Even to this day, most people from nearby Trion and Summerville believe that the ruins of Corpsewood Manor are best left alone.

The Yard Sale Dresser

Starting the first Thursday in August each year is a four day yard sale that stretches 450 miles! It begins in Gadsden, Alabama, and ends in Covington, Kentucky. Crossing four states, the merchandise includes antiques, glassware, furniture, fresh garden produce, homemade jams and jellies, and even live entertainment. With as many as 5000 vendors setting up shop, there is  usually something for everyone.

The path meanders along the top of Lookout Mountain from Gadsden to Chattanooga, Tennessee, following the Lookout Mountain Parkway. At Chattanooga it joins the 127 corridor all the way into Kentucky.

450 miles of yard sale is legendary in itself. It has also spawned additional legends, such as the following story involving a purchase along Lookout Mountain.

One Saturday a couple and their eleven year old daughter, Beth Ann, were browsing along the yard sale, not far from their home in Gadsden, Alabama. They had driven along the Lookout Mountain Parkway almost to Dogtown, and were about to turn back toward home when they spotted a battered old truck backed up close to the road. They could see that the interior of the truck bed was stacked with furniture, so they paused to check it out.

The truck itself looked like an antique. A faded sign on the side of the trailer alluded to a Jones Furniture Palace. A middle-aged couple was sitting outside the truck in lawn chairs, with a small table between them with a pitcher of ice water and several paper cups. The woman was small and  frail, but had a big welcoming smile. The man was also small, but still seemed to be agile for his age. They eagerly welcomed the young couple to look over their furniture, and the lady offered Beth Ann a cup of ice water.

The couple climbed into the back of the truck, gingerly stepping amidst the varied pieces of furniture. Meanwhile the girl had sat down in a chair next to the lady. The lady ran her hand through the young girl's long, brown hair and told her how pretty it was.

The couple was about to leave empty handed when Beth Ann ran up to them, asking them to look at an old dresser in the back of the truck. The lady had told her that she might like it, and she did. It was an antique dresser, made of solid oak, contained several small drawers, and had a large beveled mirror rising from the back of it. Nothing would do but for them to get the dresser for Beth Ann. The price was quite reasonable, so they loaded it into their pickup truck and took it home.

Beth Ann was delighted with her new dresser. She told her parents about how the lady explained that the dresser had belonged to her own daughter, several years previously.

"She said that her daughter had long red hair, and loved to sit and brush her hair in the mirror of the dresser. Then she was telling me about how her daughter got sick, and that's when you started to leave, and she told me to go look at the dresser."

Soon Beth Ann had adopted that ritual herself, and sat at the dresser each night before bedtime, watching her reflection in the mirror as she brushed and brushed her long hair.

A couple of months passed, and Beth Ann was spending more and more of her evening time in her room, sitting at the dresser and brushing her hair. Then one morning Beth Ann didn't appear for breakfast. When her mother checked her room, the bed had not been slept in, and there was no sign of Beth Ann. None of her possessions were missing, not even any of her clothes. The only thing that wasn't accounted for was Beth Ann's hairbrush. It was as if the girl had vanished into thin air.

The Gadsden police were called, but several days went by without anyone seeing or hearing anything from Beth Ann. Finally, about a week after the disappearance, a friend from school stopped by the house. She hesitatingly related a chilling tale to the parents. Judy, the best friend of Beth Ann, told them the following:

"Beth Ann said that she thought the dresser was magic or something. After a week or so of brushing her hair at the mirror, strange things began to happen. Beth Ann said that one night she was sitting there at her dresser, brushing her hair, when suddenly she became aware that the image in the mirror wasn't her. It was a girl about her age brushing her hair; only her hair was long and red. She said that the image was only there for a second, and it seemed like when she made eye contact with the other girl, the image returned to be her. She made me promise not to tell anyone, because she knew people wouldn't believe her. I didn't know what to think.

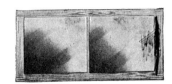

A couple days later she confided that she'd seen the strange girl again, and this time the image stayed a little longer. The other girl was quite pretty, but had a sad expression on her face. She was wearing a pale blue gown. They made eye contact for several seconds before the image returned to be Beth Ann. She said that it really spooked her at first, but for some reason it wasn't bothering her as much, and she was looking forward to seeing the red-haired girl again.

The last time I saw Beth Ann, she was really excited. She'd seen the image again, but it was quite different. Instead of the long red hair, the girl in the mirror was completely bald headed! She looked very sad, and the image stayed there for several minutes. Beth Ann said that she tried to talk to the girl, but wasn't sure whether she could hear her. Just as the image began to fade, she thought the girl beckoned to her.

And that was the last thing that we ever talked about. It was the next night when Beth Ann disappeared."

91

Beth Ann's parents didn't know what to make of Judy's story. They drove to all the towns within a fifty mile radius of Dogtown, trying to find any information on a Jones Furniture Palace, but to no avail. Nobody at any of the towns recalled there ever being such a business around them.

Beth Ann's mother began sitting in the girl's bedroom at the dresser for hours on end, staring forlornly  into the mirror. She grew more and more distraught, obsessed with the mirror. Eventually she had a nervous breakdown, and as she was taken away, was heard saying over and over, "She's in the mirror! I know she is!"

The next year, at the annual yard sale, the dresser was sold again.

The Devil's Spot

There's an area near Adamsburg, Alabama, that is most peculiar, even for Lookout Mountain. There is a circular patch of ground where absolutely nothing grows. Although there are plenty of plants of various types all around it, the circle remains completely barren. The spot is along the rugged edge of Little River Canyon, just east of Little River Falls. The remote location is not by chance, according to legend.

Some of the older folks in the region claim that the ground is barren because it belongs to the devil. They claim that many years ago there was a gypsy-like clan of people living between Blanche and Jamestown. Where they originated, nobody ever knew. One spring they all suddenly settled into the area, building their own houses and barns, and keeping much to themselves.

The clan consisted of four or five families, all of similar features, who supposedly engaged in devil worship. The females were all slender, all had long, straight black hair, and all were astonishingly beautiful. Likewise, all of the men were exceedingly handsome. However, all of the people had piercing dark eyes that would make a person uncomfortable to gaze upon them. Some said that they all possessed the "evil eye," and could hypnotize man or beast with a casual glance.

Each month, when the moon was full, these families were rumored to gather at the circle at the canyon and go through their demonic rituals. There would be eerie music, haunting chants, and wild dancing around the

circle. There were rumors of live sacrifice offerings being made to the devil during these ceremonies.

Once a man from Adamsburg was out coon hunting and chanced upon one of the ceremonies. He stayed hidden behind a tree, but got close enough to see what was happening. The hunter claimed that there was a young woman tied to a stake in the center of the circle, and the other people were chanting and dancing around her.

Suddenly, as if appearing from thin air, one of the ladies from the clan was standing beside of the hunter, and tapped him on his shoulder. He claimed that her eyes glowed as if they were on fire, and that he quickly avoided looking at them, and ran away as fast as he could go. Evil laughter seemed to follow him until he was a good half mile away.

The gossip was that others weren't as fortunate as the coon hunter, and didn't escape the evil eyes. More than one young man became enamored by the beauty of the women, and wound up missing without a trace left behind.

Eventually the clan moved away from the area as swiftly as they had arrived. Their houses and barns burned, though nobody knew if the people set them afire as they left, or whether they left because someone else set the fires.

The circular patch of ground, however, never recovered, and remains completely infertile to this very day. On nights of the full moon, sounds of chanting are frequently heard from that location. Several people have reported hearing moans and seeing shadowy figures near the circle, but as they grew closer, these things ceased, and a creepy silence followed.

The stories are that these figures are the unfortunate victims of the sacrifices to the devil during the ceremonies. Their tormented souls are destined to remain trapped at the circle forever, as it is a portal straight to hell. Their ghosts struggle in vain to escape their eternal fate.

Of course there are those who scoff at the notion of a haunted circle of ground. However, they cannot explain why nothing grows there, nor can they explain why rocks and other objects that are placed within the circle do not remain there past the following full moon.

The Anguished Prison Ghost

Portersville, Alabama, is a small community that has been a part of history for many years. It witnessed the early settlers and the infamous Trail of Tears that exiled the Cherokee Indians. It was caught in the middle of the Civil War, as armies from both sides marched repeatedly through the area

For many years there was an old house on the outskirts of Portersville that looked oddly out of place. In this seemingly tranquil community, this house had bars over all of the windows and doors. Even the upstairs windows had bars on them.

Perhaps at first glance one might have surmised that the owner was simply very wary of burglars. That, however, wasn't the reason for the bars at all.

Back in the middle part of the last century, a young couple lived in the house. Unfortunately, the man was known to drink quite heavily, particularly of the locally manufactured moonshine. One night in a drunken rage, he killed his wife.

Once sober, the man was quite remorseful, and proclaimed that he loved his wife more than himself. He blamed his actions on what he termed "bad moonshine." Nevertheless, he was sentenced to 10 years in the penitentiary.

Even after serving his time in prison, the man was

adamant that he hadn't been punished enough. That was when he installed bars on the doors and windows throughout his house. He essentially lived the rest of his life in his own prison.

Even his eventual death seemed to not have soothed his tortured soul. No tenants ever managed to stay in the house for as long as a year. They claimed that late at night there were sounds of someone pacing back and forth in the house when there was nobody to be seen. From outside the house, shadows of someone could be seen at the windows, when there was nobody inside the house.

Although the entity that haunted the house was apparently harmless, his incessant pacing and occasional moaning eventually proved too much for the tenants, and they moved out, leaving the poor man to his private prison.

Finally a new owner of the property removed all of the bars from the house. Apparently this set the spirit free, as there have not been any reports of ghostly sounds or sightings since then.

The Ghosts of Collinsville

About halfway between Gadsden and Fort Payne, Alabama, along Highway 11, is a quiet little place by the name of Collinsville. It is one of the places where one can 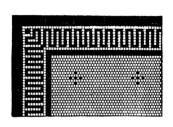 still drive down shady streets, view well preserved older homes, and breathe in a tangible air of hospitality and friendliness.

Come rain or shine, every Saturday will find Collinsville Trade Day operating in full glory on the south end of town on U.S. Highway 11. This claims to be the oldest and largest flea market in Alabama. On the surface, ghosts might well be the last thing on your mind. First impressions can be deceiving.

Collinsville was at one time in the Land of the Cherokee Nation. It lies just west of Lookout Mountain, and is nestled down in a valley, with a ridge to the west of it. Little Wills Creek flows through the middle of town, making for a beautiful, peaceful venue for most of the time.

However, this serene setting has had more than its share of tragedy and disaster, two main ingredients for ghostly tales. The center of town has virtually been destroyed by fire more than once. There have been numerous destructive floods; so many that it became accepted that every five years the town would flood.

With the high terrain on its east and west sides, and centered between the north and south forks of the Little Wills  Creek, there was no place for rain and runoff water to go except through the town. Only in recent years has major renovations alleviated this methodical flooding.

One early incident that blemishes the area is the infamous Trail of Tears, when many of the Indians were rounded up and moved west of the Mississippi. The lands that they and their ancestors had roamed for many years was deemed too valuable for Indian use, and was systematically given to the more deserving white settlers. Legend has it that this led to a curse being placed on the town that resulted in many of its disasters.

On February 2, 1900, a fire was noticed on the roof of B.A. Nowlin's general merchandise store. The store was located on the west end of Main Street. The gossip was that it began with a fire arrow, shot by an Indian figure on horseback who had ridden in from the direction of Lookout Mountain. The wind was blowing in from the west, pushing the fire and embers toward the main part of town. Before the fire could be controlled, it quickly spread to nearby wooden buildings. By the time the fire was contained, most of downtown Collinsville was lost.

As a majority of the townspeople were engaged in fighting the spreading blazes, several reported hearing the rhythmic slow beat of Indian drums coming from Lookout Mountain. The ghosts of the displaced Cherokees were restless.

Of course Collinsville has its theater ghosts, too. The first "picture show" was operated by Emory Williams. The theater was located on the north side of Main Street, near the railroad. Occasionally a train would come through during the showing of a movie, drowning out the sound, and sometimes vibrating everything in the building.

The next theater was run by Charlie Siniard. Then Millard Wever opened The Cricket Theatre in 1925. There were several incidents at this site, which were blamed on the Indian curse. The movie reels were always breaking at a critical point in the movies; there were unexplained pounding noises on the roof, and even shadows cast upon the screen that observers claimed to look like Indian warriors.

The rumor persisted that the theater was built on sacred ground to the Cherokees, and they were not happy with its use. The Cricket Theatre moved to a new building in the middle 1940s, and the incidents ceased. The theater finally closed in 1964, apparently having made peace with the Indian ghosts.

And finally there is the incident of the first bank in Collinsville. It was organized in 1902 by L. C. Harding, who promptly disappeared with all the money. One legend maintains that upon opening the vault one morning, Harding encountered the ghost of an Indian chief. The ghost demanded the money, and Harding fled in fear and panic.

A different version of this legend has Harding, himself, as the ghost. In any event, the people's money disappeared, leaving many of them destitute.

There are also stories of a local inn being haunted by the ghosts of soldiers from the Civil War. Many visitors have reported seeing and hearing soldiers marching up and down the halls. Items in rooms have been mysteriously moved around. One visitor climbed into bed one night only to discover a mini-ball between the covers. He quickly checked out.

So Collinsville is a quiet little town on the surface, but please be aware of its history. Who knows when the Indian curse may strike again?

Ghosts of Gadsden

  Gadsden, Alabama, is located at the southern end of Lookout Mountain. It has had its share of historical limelight, being an instrumental location before, during, and after the Civil War. Its many claims to fame include being the starting place of the World's Longest Yardsale near the first of August each year. The nearby Noccalula Falls Park also attracts many visitors annually, so though small, Gadsden is a bustling little town.

For some reason, Gadsden also seems to be a haven for a large number of ghosts from many different time periods. From the 1800s to the present, strange occurrences and apparitions have been common in the community. Sightings have been made at many different locations in the area, by a variety of people.

For instance, there is a Crestwood Cemetery located where a former cotton plantation once set back in the 1800s. While visiting the graves of family or friends, eyewitnesses have caught brief glimpses of elements of a slave-hanging. Assorted people have reported seeing men, horses, and dogs, as well as the unfortunate victim, appearing throughout portions of the cemetery.

Loud noises and shadowy figures are recurring events at the Mountain View Hospital in Gadsden. Sometimes these come from seemingly vacant rooms, and are also observed in the backyard of the hospital late at night. Several workers at the hospital as well as patients and visitors have reported hearing and seeing these

strange incidents. There have been times that patients have reported someone coming into their room late at night, then simply disappearing into thin air, or inexplicably vaporizing through the outside wall.

The Gadsden Public Library has its own ghost. In this case, the founder of the library is often heard walking about, and has occasionally been sighted on the premises.

Hinds Road, in Gadsden, runs between Noccalula Mountain and the Dwight Mill Village. Supposedly a witch once lived along this road, and mysterious things still occur in the dark of night. Orbs of light have been frequently seen hovering and darting about the road. These orbs have even been photographed by ghost investigators, but nobody has been able to explain their origin.

Forrest Middle School of Gadsden is named after the famous Civil War General. His ghost is reported to regularly be seen at the school, with weird things happening, particularly in the 6th grade basement.

Gadsden also has the infamous Haunted Bridge legend. Many years ago, a young couple lived near the bridge. After an argument one night, the lady left with their baby, walking out into the night. Before long the man began feeling remorseful, hitched up his horses to his buggy and went out looking for his wife and baby. Hearing him approach, the lady emerged from her spot of refuge beneath the bridge. Unfortunately, her sudden appearance spooked the horses and they inadvertently knocked the lady and baby down into Black Creek, with both of them drowning.

Since that time, people have reported seeing a woman dressed in black pacing back and forth across the bridge, as if in search of something. When approached, she vanishes.

People have also reported hearing a woman's scream, carriage wheels rolling along, an infant crying, or a man cursing when there was nothing else around to cause these noises. In more recent times, a man dressed in black has seen standing on the bridge, staring into the water below. When anyone nears him, he slowly vanishes into thin air.

Supposedly, the house where this couple lived is still standing, but nobody has been able to live in it for any length of time because of "strange things happening."

Noccalula Falls

  Noccalula Falls Park, at Gadsden, Alabama, is a stunningly beautiful park located on State Highway 211. Open daily, it proudly boasts of many historical sites worth visiting. It is located at the southern end of Lookout Mountain, and is visited by many tourists each year. These visitors are treated to spectacular views, as well as  evidence of Indian inhabitants and other life centuries ago.

  There is a gorge trail with caves and Indian carvings, a decrepit dam, an old aboriginal fort, and many carvings from the Civil War period. The entire park is surrounded by a huge botanical garden, with thousands of azaleas presenting a most picturesque setting. Walking trails traverse the garden, or it can be viewed by a train ride, which also passes through a replica pioneer village.

But foremost, the park is home to a beautiful waterfall for which the place is named. The spectacular one hundred foot high Noccalula Falls was named for an Indian girl, the victim of an unfortunate love match.

According to the legend, the Indian girl fell in love with a young brave in her tribe. Unfortunately, her father had already chosen another brave to be her husband, and according to their custom, she had to follow the wishes of her father.

The girl was naturally heartbroken, and rather than betray her true love, she climbed to the top of the falls and threw herself into the rushing waters, plunging to her death in the churning pool far below. Grief-stricken at the loss of his daughter, Noccalula, the father named the falls after her.

Since that tragedy, many people through the years have reported sighting an Indian maiden carefully walking along the top of the falls. There have also been many reports of people seeing her form in the misty spray at the base of the falls. They claim that the apparition slowly materializes as it rises from the water, then fades quickly into the plunging water of the falls themselves. The entire incident only takes about a second, but it has been described similarly by many different people over the years. It seems that the young maiden is still haunting the premises.

The LaFayette Tunnel Spirits

Since 1835, the county seat of Walker County, Georgia, has been LaFayette, home to 6700 people in the 2000 census. Its first courthouse survived a bloody battle

during the Civil War only to burn in 1883, destroying records for the previous 50 years. A replacement building was constructed that same year, but it had iron vaults to fireproof the future records.

Another courthouse was built in 1918, and was considered to be the premier courthouse in Georgia at the time. The site of the former courthouse was converted into a public park, designed around a

Confederate monument. The park later was paved to become downtown parking, but the Confederate monument remains today.

Originally home to many Cherokee Indians, LaFayette was the site of Fort Cumming, one of the Cherokee Removal Forts, housing the Indians prior to their forced march to Oklahoma. The site of the fort is now where the present day water plant stands.

About five miles west of LaFayette is Pigeon Mountain Wildlife Management Area, featuring several thousand acres that are ideal for hiking, hunting, horseback riding, and exploring many caves in the area. There are also rock cliffs and outcrops for the aspiring rock climbers, and the Hood Overlook is well known by experienced hang gliders.

Of special interest to many are the nearby series of old railroad tunnels left over from the mining heyday of the area in the 1900s. Some of these tunnels have been blocked off to discourage entry, but several can still be explored. One particular tunnel has had more than its fair share of unexplained incidents over the years.

First reports of possible hauntings emerged during the 1960s. A troop of young explorers from a church group entered the tunnel right after dark one night. Almost immediately they began seeing lights moving around ahead of them. They assumed that it was another group of explorers, but suddenly the lights vanished. The group continued to the other end of the tunnel without any indication that anyone else had been ahead of them.

Then they noticed lights behind them in the tunnel again. Retracing their steps, again they saw the lights vanish, and they emerged at the original end of the tunnel without seeing anyone.

Lights in the tunnel became a common occurrence, with many reports in subsequent years. Legend has it that several men were killed during the construction of the tunnel when a portion of the ceiling collapsed on them. The lights now seen in the tunnel are from the lanterns of the dead men trying to find their way out.

Another story claims that there was a train collision in the tunnel, killing the engineers of both trains. The lights now sighted represent warning lights of an on-coming train that never appears.

Lending credibility to this version are the occasional reports that the sound of an approaching steam locomotive often accompanies the lights. Of course the train never arrives, and the sound fades away with the lights.

In more recent years more than one explorer has reported seeing a lantern floating in the air, accompanied by a moaning sound. One individual claimed that the lantern completely circled him before appearing to vanish into the wall of the tunnel.

Civil War Sentry

   During the Civil War there was much commotion along
Lookout Mountain. There were popular trails along which
both armies marched into battle. There were also vital
railroad lines utilized to ship both men and supplies to
the armies. Controlling the use of the trails and rails
became
extremely
important to
both the
North and the
South.

   At various
times during
the conflict
between the states, either the Northern or the
Southern armies controlled these supply routes and the
surrounding areas. There were some particular vantage
points along the mountain, primarily due to the extended

view they provided of the nearby terrain. Some such areas were near the present day community of Cloudland.

High along the ridge of the mountain the viewer has a panoramic view for miles around. These scenic overlooks of today served the armies well during the Civil War.

There was one particular spot located off one of the main trails that was ideal for the armies. It provided widespread coverage of the valley on the eastern side of Lookout Mountain far below. This site was noteworthy for a couple of important reasons.

First of all, the secluded location provided a fantastic view of a major route traveled by the Northern armies. Second of all, since the site wasn't obvious from the nearby trail, most of the Yankee soldiers were never aware of its existence.

Alerted to its strategic location by the local Southern sympathizers, the Rebel soldiers took great advantage throughout the war of both of these facts, and frequently had a sentry posted there, keeping tabs on the movements of the Union armies.

So hidden was the site that often a Southern soldier would stay there even when the Northern armies were in control of the immediate area. Their creative means of communication consisted of the oft-scoffed old smoke and mirrors scheme.

The hidden sentry used a mirror to flash signals to his colleagues far below, or to a ridge across the way. At night he could use a small lantern to send signals. At other times, when the enemy was not close behind him, he could even send smoke signals. The Northern armies, even if they saw the smoke, often disregarded it, thinking it was Indians.

As the story goes, a Rebel soldier was posted at the hidden site when the Northerners took control of the surrounding area. Instead of passing on through, they remained camped there for several weeks. Typically, the sentry assigned to the secret spot was sick or wounded. Not being able to travel very well, he could still contribute by spying from above. This particular soldier had been wounded and was already weak. Trapped in his place of hiding, and not wanting to give away the secret location, the Southern soldier ran out of food and water, eventually starving to death.

According to the legend, the ghost of this Rebel soldier still resides high up on the

mountain, continuing to man the spying location. He continues to watch the valley below, and sends signals to comrades who no longer exist. Frequently at night a faint light appears up on the mountain. Unexplained bright flashes of light occur in broad daylight. There have even been puffs of smoke observed drifting upward from that location. Subsequent investigations have failed to find a source for any of these occurrences.

The local explanation is that the ghost of the Rebel soldier remains at his post to this day, faithfully fulfilling his duty, in death as he did in life.

Peeping Tom Ghost

Leesburg, Alabama, is home to some of the most breath-taking views of all Lookout Mountain. From atop large rock formations the visitor can see Rome, Georgia, to the east, and Weisner Mountain to the south. The town of Gadsden lies to the west, with a sparkling display of lights as darkness falls. Speaking of falls, nearby is the Yellow  Creek Falls which drop 100 feet into beautiful Weiss Lake. Walking, hiking, fishing, and boating are some of the activities available to visitors to the area.

Of course there are ghosts, as well. The most popular one haunts a local bed and breakfast inn. The facility was built on the site where an old log general store had been many years previously. This general store was known as "Old Joe's General" by its regular customers. Since it was the only store around, the local people had no choice but to patronize it.

The proprietor, named "Joe," of course, knew everybody around the Leesburg community. His wife had died young, and with no kids, Joe lived alone in the back portion of the store. Old Joe was a large man, bald-headed, and almost always had this disarming, big, toothy grin on his face.

With this friendly façade, Joe quickly made acquaintances, and folks said that he knew everybody around. Not only did he know them, he knew their kinfolk, their friends, their business, and probably the location of their birthmarks. You see, Old Joe was what could be termed as rather nosey.

He had a way of prying all types of information out of a person, especially the things that people had just as soon keep private. Secrets were difficult to keep from Joe. Without meaning to spill the beans on themselves, Joe had a way of wrangling the most personal information out of his customers.

Therefore, with the passing through his store of most of the people in the community, Joe was a wealth of gossip, rumors, and hearsay.

Nobody made a quick trip to Joe's store, as he would invariably engage them in a drawn out conversation, poking around in their business, as well as informing them of the current community gossip.

This was a good thing and a bad thing. It was good because a trip to Joe's store was the equivalent of reading our modern day newspapers, and it kept the people informed of all the latest local news. It was bad in that there was no censorship, and frequently information was spread that folks wished had not been.

Eventually his wealth of information and his proclivity of dispensing it got Old Joe in trouble. There were rumors concerning the goings and comings of a circuit rider preacher, who visited Leesburg regularly two times a month, and a couple of the locally prominent married ladies. Naturally this was an exceptionally juicy bit of scandalous gossip; too juicy in the end.

Late one night Old Joe's general store burned completely to the ground, and Joe's body was found in the smoking ruins. According to unconfirmed rumors, Joe had been shot several times and was dead before the fire began. According to the local sheriff, however, Joe died accidentally in the fire, period.

In either case, Joe's demise was beneficial to the reputations of the two local ladies, one of which just so happened to be married to the sheriff. The preacher found a calling at a distant community and was not seen in the area again.

Years later the hotel was built on the site where the general store had burned. Almost immediately there were reports of peculiar happenings. There was one particular room on the back side of the hotel where these things occurred, as lady guests began complaining of quite unsettling incidents.

Investigations were in vain, and the incidents have continued through the  years, with seldom much time going by without a lady complaining of seeing the face of a peeping tom at her bedroom or bathroom window. He is always described as bald-headed with a big grin on his face.

Usually the face disappears as soon as the startled ladies notice it and are frightened. One lady reported that she pretended not to see him, and the face remained watching her for at least twenty minutes. When she finally approached the window, the face disappeared.

The problem is that these windows where he is seen are at least twenty feet off the ground, with no easy means of being accessible, except by ladder. Of course there is never a ladder found there. Apparently Old Joe's ghost continues his inquisitive ways long after his untimely death.

Hangover Hank

Back in the early 1950s, there was a man who was often seen around the towns of Alpine and Menlo, Georgia. Some said he was a beggar, some said he was "born a few bricks shy of a load," some said that he became that way  after a long illness with a high fever, and some said that he was a shell-shocked victim of World War II. In any event, the man became what almost every small town used to refer to as the "town character." He was called, "Hangover Hank," which explains a lot about his demeanor and the people who named him.

Some towns were blessed with several such characters. These people, not quite right in the head for whatever reason, relied upon doing odd jobs and the kindness of locals to provide their means of living. Nowadays these people seem to be in institutions, cared for by government organizations, or, in my case, are distant relatives. Back then, however, they generally roamed around town, looking for small jobs or handouts. Usually they were accepted by the local people, frequently given free access to sporting events, and sometimes

simply "seen about" by good hearted townsfolk.

Both Alpine and Menlo are quaint little mountain towns where many of the locals have lived there for generations. Most people know all of their neighbors, and this has generated a family-type relationship among the inhabitants. They are accustomed to looking out for each other in times of need, and without another thought, both towns more or less adopted Hank and accepted him into their community.

Hangover Hank used to ramble along the two and a half miles between Alpine and Menlo during all hours of the day and night. At night he often carried a small lantern with him, swinging it along as he stumbled on his way. Hank was in the habit of talking to himself or singing as he walked along, so you usually had a little warning that he was approaching.

As far as anyone knew, Hank actually lived in a small cave between the towns, though nobody ever admitted seeing the cave. At times some of the younger folks tried to follow Hank home, but he always seemed to sense their presence, and refused to lead them to his cavern.

Hank became an institution at both of the towns, and could always be counted on to appear at any ball game, public picnic, singing, or political rally. He was never unruly, although some folks would try to get him riled up. He'd just fix them with a glassy stare until they gave up and shut up.

Hank wore an old dark brown coat, summer or winter, rain or shine. Nobody could ever remember seeing him without it. The coat and Hank seemed to have appeared at the same time.

One morning after a particularly dark and stormy night, a park ranger on his way to work discovered Hank's body along the road between the 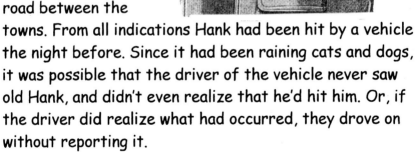 towns. From all indications Hank had been hit by a vehicle the night before. Since it had been raining cats and dogs, it was possible that the driver of the vehicle never saw old Hank, and didn't even realize that he'd hit him. Or, if the driver did realize what had occurred, they drove on without reporting it.

Nevertheless, Hank was deceased. Since his body had been found closer to Menlo, that's where he was buried. Citizens from both towns donated money to pay for the cost of his funeral, and everyone thought that was the end of it.

Hank, however, refused for it all to end like that. For the ensuing decades, Hank is still occasionally seen wandering along the road. Sometimes he is headed toward Menlo, and at other times he is going toward Alpine. Invariably he is seen at night, and he is always swinging that lantern high above his head.

Those who have seen this vision and stopped, consistently report that Hank disappears as soon as their vehicle stops moving. Many relate that they still hear a humming sound, but never can tell where it's coming from.

Naturally this has been quite startling to many travelers along the road who haven't heard of the Hank legend. Many of the local folk have witnessed old Hank's ghost, and have grown accustomed to the incidents. Because Hank never arrived home that night, his ghost seems doomed to continually search for the path to his cavern.

Sequoyah Caverns Spirits

Sequoyah Caverns is a major tourist attraction at Valley Head, Alabama. It is located a little northeast of Fort Payne, just off Highway 11, and not far from Interstate 59. Surrounded by rolling hills and fertile pastures, the

area outside the caverns is as picturesque as the treasures inside.

The caverns get their name from the Cherokee Indian Chief Sequoyah. Chief Sequoyah is also credited with creating the Cherokee alphabet. He fought alongside Andrew Jackson and Sam Houston in the War of 1812, and around 1820 settled in Willstown, just south of the Sequoyah Caverns.

The caverns have been owned and operated by the same family for generations. There is a campground and picnic area for the visitors, as well as farmland with many animals, including goats and deer.

The more spectacular delights are waiting for the visitors inside the caverns. Guided tours take the guests to the reflecting pools of the underground lakes, mirroring the many beautiful cave formations that are spread abundantly throughout the caverns. According to legends, there could be other things lurking inside the caverns, as well.

There are many stories told of unusual and weird adventures in the caverns. Inexplicable sounds of moans and wailing have frequently been reported by those venturing deep in the caverns. Lights going out for no reason, and then coming back on again have happened time and time  again. This light problem seems to have always occurred along the same path each time. Due to this and the story of a young explorer's experience several years ago causes most of the current adventurers to always pack an extra light when they enter the caverns.

The story relates how this young female explorer had traveled deep in the cavern one day when she tripped and fell. She wasn't injured, but her flashlight was broken, leaving her in complete darkness. Before she had time to get totally despaired at her situation, she became aware that a faint glow was approaching her.

Astonished, she saw a young Indian man in the glow. Without a word, he slowly drew near, and then motioned for her to follow him. They traveled along the path in silence until, eventually, the lady saw the daylight from the cavern opening up ahead. Overjoyed, she turned to thank her rescuer, but the Indian and the glow had totally vanished. She stumbled out of the cavern, completely bewildered by the incident, and at a total loss to explain her good fortune.

The closest thing to a scientific rationalization was that she had hit her head when she fell, and miraculously found her own way back to the cavern entrance  in an addled state induced by the blow and had simply imagined the Indian guide.

Another explanation, which ties in more fittingly with the local legends, is that one of the Cherokee warriors who had perished in the caverns while hiding from the Trail of Tears roundup was her guide. He is one of several Indian ghosts who have inhabited the caverns for many years, and he took pity on the explorer and guided her to the safety that he never found. This is only one instance of these Indian ghosts being seen at various places in the caverns.

There is one chamber located deep in the caverns that is often referred to the Chamber of Grief. Visitors to this chamber consistently report noticing a chilling sensation upon entry, and then feeling an overwhelming feeling of depression, which intensifies the longer they remain there. Due to the consistent uneasiness felt by the guests, this

chamber is often omitted on the guided tours.

When the Indians were being rounded up and detained prior to the forced Trail of Tears march to Oklahoma, some of them managed to sneak away and hide in the caverns. Some of the Indians were already sick, and due to a lack of food, several of them died. They were buried in one of the chambers deep inside the cavern.

Due to the belief that a burial must be witnessed by the gods, the unfortunate souls of the Indians buried in the cavern were trapped there. There they are doomed to hopelessly wander aimlessly around the caverns, not wanting to leave their remains, but unable to meet the gods. These spirits are sometimes seen and/or heard by the people exploring the caverns.

The Phantom Rider

Cloudland Canyon State Park is located on the northwestern edge of Lookout Mountain in Georgia. Nearby towns are Trenton and Cooper Heights. Chattanooga, Tennessee, lies to the north and a little east. Starting with picturesque rolling hills the terrain abruptly changes to the rugged beauty of a gorge carved by many years of wind and water forces.

The approach to the park is a treacherous two-lane highway, and the winding road has many switchbacks, necessitating focused caution by the drivers. There have been many vehicles that have bounced down the sides of the canyon over the years. Some of these were by accident, but a few years ago a truck theft ring used the canyon to dispose of their stolen vehicles.

The park actually straddles a deep ravine forged into the mountain by Daniel Creek. It has two stunning waterfalls at the bottom of the gorge, and has spectacular views both from the picnic area and the rim of the canyon high above. The park varies in altitude from 800 feet to almost 2000 feet at the canyon rim.

Originally know as Sitton Gulch, it was renamed to its present name when purchased by Georgia around 1939 and made into a state park.

As well as the magnificent scenic beauty, there are also multiple hiking opportunities. Some of these should only be undertaken by the more experienced hikers, as the terrain is sometimes very rugged.

Beauty and exercise are not the only features of the park, however. There have been many reports over the years of sightings of the ghosts of the Indians who first roamed the canyon. This area was a popular hunting and camping area for those Native Americans, too.

One particular ghost seems to be the most frequently observed by park visitors. This ghost is an Indian warrior who patrols the park on horseback, and his appearances have been reported for many years. Some people think the ghost haunts the area, while others claim that he is simply protecting them.

The Indian ghost was first reported by campers. They saw the figure on horseback positioned at a rocky outcropping high on the mountain above them. He appeared just as the last remnants of daylight were fading away. The Indian and his horse stood motionless until the enveloping darkness obscured them. Over the years, many campers in that same area have reported the identical sightings.

Some claimed to have climbed to the spot where they saw the figures when daylight came. They observed tracks of a shoeless horse at the spot, but no trace of any tracks coming or leaving the site.

In more recent years, the ghost seems to have gotten braver. There have been reports that campers both heard and observed the rider moving through the campgrounds late at night. The next day they reported seeing hoof prints around their tents, but none leading into or away from the camp.

Apparently the ghost means no harm, just either curious as to the campers, or, as some like to think, looking out for their welfare.

The Ghosts of Chickamauga

Nestled in the northwest corner of Georgia, at the base of Lookout Mountain, and just south of Chattanooga, Tennessee, is Chickamauga. 2800 acres of this area was set aside around 1930 as a national park to commemorate its importance during the Civil War. Today it is  one of the most popular sites for visitors interested in the history of the War Between the States. One of the more famous and deadly battles of the entire Civil War was fought there.

The Battle of Chickamauga was named after the Chickamauga Creek which flowed nearby. On September

19-20, 1863, 150,000 soldiers of the Northern and Southern armies took part in a bloody battle that left 35,000 dead.

Prior to the battle, Union General Rosecrans had his headquarters in the town at the Gordon Lee Mansion, completed in 1847 and still standing today. During and after the battle, the home was used to care for many of the wounded soldiers. After the battle ended, several Northern doctors remained there attending to the wounded soldiers who were not fit to travel. There is a spring in the town, Crawfish Spring, where many of the parched and wounded soldiers of both sides drank. That spring remains active to this day and is a popular spot regularly visited by tourists to the area.

Due to the rugged terrain and heavily wooded area, many soldiers became lost and separated from their units during the battle. Communication was almost non-existent, and orders from the leaders had difficulty reaching the troops. Much of the fighting was chaotic, consisting of a great deal of hand-to-hand combat. It was an expensive battle for both sides, wiping out entire regiments. When the fighting ended, the Confederates had control of the area. It was destined to be the last major battle the Southern armies would win.

As darkness fell across the battlefield on the second day and the shooting faded away, women were seen searching the battlefield by lantern light for their kinfolk. Supposedly there are eerie lights still seen across the area, along with moaning, wailing, and cries for help from the victims, and sobbing sounds of grief from the women. The spirits seemed doomed to forever roam the battlegrounds with their lanterns, searching for, and in some cases finding, their dead or wounded relatives.

Many of the dead Union soldiers lay where they fell for more than two months after the battle before they were buried. The  logistics of dealing with that many corpses were staggering. It was not feasible to provide caskets in that quantity, so the bodies were simply placed in the ground, usually where they had fallen. Rows of graves were eventually dug all around the area, each grave holding multiple bodies. With no markers to represent the location of the graves, bodies are still occasionally uncovered by maintenance and construction crews working in the area to this day.

Years after the Civil War ended, a training camp was established on the old battlefield to prepare men for the Spanish-American War. The camp seemed ill-fated, as disease ran rampant, and many more men died there. This only added to the many deaths associated with the grounds.

There were even more deaths in subsequent years, as the sprawling park has been the scene of many murders, suicides, and the occasional accidental deaths. It has also been a dumping ground for the bodies of victims killed elsewhere. With this gruesome history, there is no wonder that there are many reports of ghostly activity in the area.

One story involves the planned murder of a husband by his wife and her boyfriend. They lured him into the park and attacked him with knives. The man escaped and ran screaming through the park, finally rescued by park rangers with the would-be killers in pursuit. Visitors to the park continue to report seeing and hearing blood-curdling screams and a bleeding figure stumble across their camps or in the roadways, only to suddenly vanish into thin air.

There seem to be many ghosts and spirits roaming the fields around Chickamauga. Campers frequently report hearing men moaning and crying out when there is no one there. There is frequently a feeling of being watched from the woods. Some see tree limbs moving with no explanation, one visitor reported seeing an entire squadron of ragged soldiers stumbling by, and several have reported seeing a horse pass by with a headless rider on board.

There is a "lady in white" ghost who has been sighted many times over the years. Legend has it that she was the wife or lover of a soldier lost in the Civil War battle, and her spirit is still searching for his spirit. Apparently she still searches in vain.

Another popular story involves the Chickamauga Monster, or "Old Green Eyes," as it is called. This entity has been around for many years, and is still repeatedly seen by both visitors and camp rangers, too.

One version claims that it is the ghost of a Confederate soldier who had his head blown off during the battle. His headless body was buried, and now he continues to prowl the area searching for his head.

Another version has the creature being a beast, not a human, and that it was present long before the Civil War. There are supposedly Indian legends describing the critter consistent with the present day reports. It is depicted as standing upright, taller than the average man, with long, unruly hair, fangs, and the glowing green eyes for which it is named.

Both visitors and park employees claim to have witnessed the green eyes coming straight toward them, accompanied by snarls and growling sounds, but nobody has actually been attacked by the creature. At least they haven't been attacked and lived to tell about it.

There have also been strange events reported at Wilder Tower. This monument of the Civil War battle is a stone structure that stands 85 feet high. It was constructed in 1903 by the men who had served under Colonel John T. Wilder at Chickamauga.

When the tower was erected, souvenirs of the war were sealed into the cornerstone. In 1976 the cornerstone was opened, and, although there were no signs that it had been disturbed, the items inside that had been placed there in 1903 had vanished.

There have also been several accidents at the tower, and naturally, at least one death. Some say there are ghosts who stand guard at the tower, discouraging anyone from getting too close to it.

With so many tragic deaths associated with this area over the past two hundred years, it is a fertile location for ghostly entities. For those inclined toward hunting for spirits in haunted places, Chickamauga is a prime destination.

The Party Ghost

 A short time after the Civil War ended, there was a
family that moved near the present community of Rogers,
Alabama, from a northern state. The man of the family
was given control of a local cotton gin as a reward for his
loyal service
with the Union
army. This
practice was too
common during
that era, and
the people
moving into the
southern areas
claiming so-

called "spoils of the war" were known as carpetbaggers.
The gin was prosperous, so soon the family was quite well
to do.
 This carpetbagger family was named Henson. One of the
Henson daughters turned eighteen about a year after

moving into the community. Nothing would do but for her to have a grand party to celebrate that important birthday. Old Mr. Henson spared no expense for the party, as he tended to spoil his daughters with his newfound wealth. There were plans for an elaborate outdoor celebration on the grounds of the Henson mansion, and many guests were invited.

Unfortunately, on the day of the birthday party storm clouds moved in, bringing rain, thunder and lightning. No sooner had the party gotten underway, than it was canceled by the downpour.

The Henson girl, irate at the interruption of her day in the spotlight, looked out in anger from her upstairs bedroom window, despondent at the ruined remains of her party on the lawn. Just as she shouted a curse at the weather, a bolt of lightning streaked down and struck the girl, knocking her across the room and killing her instantly.

Incredibly, the shadowy form of the girl was imprinted on the bedroom wall. The grief-stricken family immediately had the wall painted, covering the girl's imprint. A day later, the mark returned. Subsequent painting was also in vain, as the girl's form continued to emerge within a day or two of being covered.

Amidst rumors of other strange things happening, the Henson family sold out and moved back up north. The next people who dwelled in the house only stayed a couple of weeks before they, too, moved away.

The local gossip was that the spirit of the dead girl still haunted that bedroom. Rumors abounded that the occupants of the bedroom could not sleep because of the Henson girl's ghost. There would be moaning sounds and curses coming from the wall where the imprint refused to be covered. Footsteps could be heard pacing back and forth across the room at all hours of the

day or night. From outside in the yard, the young girl's silhouette could frequently be seen at the window of the bedroom.

Three different families followed the Hensons in living in the house, but none stayed longer than a few weeks. The house remained vacant for several months, with the ghostly rumors keeping the house from being purchased. Then one year to the day of the girl's birthday party, out of a clear sky, a bolt of lightning struck the house, and it burned to the ground.

For many years after that the land was clear, used primarily as pastureland. Modern day progress eventually arrived, and a gas station has been built on the spot.

There have been several instances of people hearing strange sounds, seeing shadows, and having weird sensations in the lady's bathroom of that station. Perhaps the Henson girl's ghost is still there, cursing the ruination of her eighteenth birthday party.

EPILOGUE

While researching for this book, I was intrigued in discovering that almost every community has at least one event that can be described as ghostly or unexplainable. Also, it seems that a majority of people has experienced something that fell beyond their normal span of belief. If they haven't, they know someone, or someone's cousin's friend, who has.

In my own family there have been several incidents that are difficult to explain. I began this book with a story of my sister seeing a ghost, but that is only one experience.

Many years ago another relative's daughter was going on a bus trip to visit her mother's sister. This trip was going to take a couple of days. The mother gave her daughter traveling money, and bid her safe travel. That night the mother dreamed that she saw a hand reaching into her daughter's purse and taking the money. The dream was so real to the mother that she went to the telegraph office the next morning and wired replacement money to her sister. When the daughter arrived at her destination, she was distraught at having lost her money. She was then astonished to learn that her mother had already sent money to the aunt to replace the stolen funds.

Several years ago I had a little white cat that followed every footstep that I made. The cat was my shadow. She was always at my feet or in my lap. After she died, I still caught brief glimpses of the cat for several days. It was as if the cat wasn't quite ready to leave me.

What is the meaning of these types of events? To me it means that there is much more to this world around us than we normally perceive. Is it possible that so many witnesses to these events over the years are all wrong? Do they all have some type of collective hallucinations? Perhaps there are logical explanations for all of the phenomena mentioned in these tales. Or perhaps we still have much to learn about this world and its inhabitants.

Author's Bio

 I was born and raised in Tennessee, then farmed out to Texas for many years. Thus, I have managed to acquire many character flaws that can be attributed to both states. I also have had the misfortune of working with computers for several decades, picking up many more peculiarities inherent with that association. In spite of all that, my outward appearance is that of a semi-well-adjusted person. Having paid attention during brief spans of my life, however, I have somehow retained the following observations:
 Never trust your brain to think logically.
 Never trust your eyes to see correctly.
 Never trust your heart to believe objectively.

Those viewpoints served me well in writing this book.

To Order Copies

Please send me _____ copies of *Ghosts of Lookout Mountain* at $11.95 each plus $3.50 shipping on the first book, and $.75 shipping each additional book.
(Make checks payable to Quixote Press.)

Name _____

Street _____

City _____ State ____ Zip_____

Quixote Press
3544 Blakslee Street
Wever, IA 52658
1-800-571-2665

To Order Copies

Please send me _____ copies of *Ghosts of Lookout Mountain* at $11.95 each plus $3.50 shipping on the first book, and $.75 shipping each additional book.
(Make checks payable to Quixote Press.)

Name _____

Street _____

City _____ State ____ Zip_____

Quixote Press
3544 Blakslee Street
Wever, IA 52658
1-800-571-2665